Series 497

Freed

The Discontented Pony

by NOEL BARR

with illustrations by P. B. HICKLING

Publishers: Ladybird Books Ltd . Loughborough
© Ladybird Books Ltd (formerly Wills & Hepworth Ltd) 1951
Printed in England

THE DISCONTENTED PONY

Once upon a time there was a pony called Merrylegs. He was a handsome little fellow, with a nose as soft as velvet, and a brown coat that shone like a polished chestnut. He lived on a farm, where he had many friends, a nice warm stable, plenty of food, and green fields in which to run and kick up his heels. His two very special friends were a white calf called Daisy, and a pink pig called Squeaker.

Now I am sure you will agree with me that Merrylegs had everything to make him happy, but I am sorry to tell you that he was a very discontented little pony. When he was a baby his mother told him, with great pride, that his great-great-grandfather had been a race horse. At the time Merrylegs paid very little attention to what his mother said, but as he began to grow up he remembered it more and more often, and at last decided that he was much too well-born to work.

So, Merrylegs became more and more discontented, and grumbled when he had to deliver the milk, or take the farmer to market, or the farmer's wife out visiting.

One fine day the farmer harnessed Merrylegs to the little cart, and got ready to go to market. In the cart he put new-laid eggs, butter and cheese, and red roses out of his garden. The brown pony grumbled to himself as usual, and fidgeted so much that the farmer had to call his little son to hold the reins until he was ready.

At last they were off, and Merrylegs trotted down the road at a good pace. The sun was shining, birds were singing, and the farmer whistled a jolly little tune.

As they drew near to the market town, the pony and the farmer heard sounds of cheerful music, and as they drove into the market square Merrylegs looked about him in astonishment. It was Fair Day, and there were some swing boats, a roundabout, and a coconut shy. Merrylegs pricked up his ears.

This was going to be fun, and he was very pleased indeed when the farmer stopped right in the market place, took the eggs and the butter and the cheese and the roses out of the cart, and disappeared down a nearby street.

There were people everywhere, and Merrylegs had never seen so many children in his life. Some were flying up into the air in swing boats, shouting and laughing; some were whizzing round on the round-about, with music playing as they went, and

quite a number of them had bought coloured balloons from a little old woman, and were running about holding them on long strings. Presently a man set up a Punch and Judy show, and Merrylegs enjoyed it tremendously. Punch made him laugh, and he was very sorry when the performance was over.

It was then that he really noticed the roundabout. He saw to his great surprise that the children were riding—not on chairs, or seats, as he had thought—but on horses. And what horses!

These were lordly creatures, with proud, flashing eyes, and wide nostrils. Their long manes and tails floated out behind them, their fore-feet pawed the air, and they had coats of scarlet, with here and there a touch of gold.

Merrylegs had never even imagined that such wonderful creatures existed. He stood quite still, his neck stretched out, his eyes filled with admiration. Suddenly he struck the hard road with his hoof, so that a spark flew into the air, and nodded his head in a lively fashion.

"Of course!" he said to himself. "Of course, that is where I should be!"

"That is the life for me! That is how the great-great-grandson of a race horse should live! I will join those shining horses on their gilded platform; they will be only too ready to welcome me when they hear about my great-great-grandfather."

At that moment the farmer came back, and he and Merrylegs set out on their homeward journey.

As soon as the little pony was turned loose in the field he galloped to the hedge, for he knew Daisy would be in the field beyond. Sure enough, she came running up as soon as she heard Merryleg's little whinny.

"Hullo," she said, panting a little. "Did you have a good time? How lucky you are, I wish I could be driven to market!"

"Lucky!" snorted Merrylegs. "I don't think I'm at all lucky! Listen to me, Daisy, I'm going to leave the farm to-night."

"Going to leave the farm!" said Daisy, in a very surprised voice. "Whatever for?" and she moved closer to the hedge, so that she could see Merrylegs more clearly.

Merrylegs told her all about the roundabout horses, and how he had made up his mind to become one of them. The little white calf looked sad. "Don't go, Merrylegs," she said, "stay with us, Squeaker and I would miss you very much."

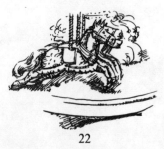

But the brown pony was determined to go, and when he met Squeaker he told him all about the plan.

" Don't go, Merrylegs," grunted Squeaker. "Forget all about those silly red horses, and stay here with us. Daisy and I would feel lonely without you." But Merrylegs would take advice from no one, though later on, when he said good-bye to Daisy and Squeaker, he felt very unhappy indeed, and wished he could take them with him.

Late that night, when all was quiet, and the lights in the farmhouse had been put out, Merrylegs pushed his way through a gap in the hedge, and stood on the road. "Goodbye to the farm!" he neighed softly, and then he trotted away towards the town. It was not quite dark, for the moon was shining, but it was very quiet and still. Once he met a dog running along the road, and it startled him; but the dog was in a hurry, and only called out "Good-night" as it hurried by.

At last Merrylegs reached the market square, and here he found everything very silent and deserted. The lively swing boats were quiet; not one of them moved. The coconut shy was empty, and the round-about, with its scarlet horses, was deserted.

Merrylegs stood in the shadow of a wall, and waited for a moment. He looked round; there was no one about. He listened; and there wasn't a sound. He picked his way as quietly as he could to the round-about and, with a beating heart, went up to one of the horses he admired so much.

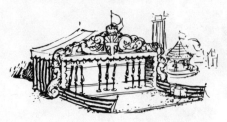

"Excuse me," he said as politely as he could, "do you think you could move up a little and make room for me? My great-great-grandfather was a race horse, and I would like to join you and your relations."

The scarlet horse said nothing. Merrylegs looked at him, gave a little cough, and waited. Still the scarlet horse was silent, so Merrylegs moved on to the next one.

"Excuse me," he said as politely as before. "Excuse me, will you be so kind as to move up and make room for me?"

" My great-great-grandfather was a race horse, and I would like to become one of you."

But the second horse said nothing. Merrylegs could see his brilliant eyes shining in the moonlight, and wondered why he didn't speak, but when he had tried another horse, and after that another one, he decided that they must all be asleep, and that they must sleep with their eyes open.

"I mustn't disturb them," he thought. "I will wait until daylight, they will wake up then." And he moved over to stand by

what looked like a little painted house on wheels.

For some time the brown pony waited patiently, and he was almost asleep when the sound of a voice coming from the caravan, woke him.

"Jim," it said, "Jim, what's that funny noise outside? It sounds like someone snoring!"

"Nothing, go to sleep," another voice, a rather muffled one, answered.

" But Jim, there's really something there, do go and see what it is," came the first voice again. Merrylegs was just going to move away, when there was a grunt, and a man came out of the caravan. He was dressed only in shirt and trousers, and his hair stood on end.

" My stars," he said. " Hi, Mary! You were right! It's a pony! I wonder where he came from. I'll tie him to the wheel here!" And the man fastened him up securely, and went back into the caravan.

"What a good thing they heard me," the pony said to himself. "It can only mean they are going to make me into a roundabout horse, as the man has tied me up so securely. Just exactly what I want. I am really very lucky." And then he heard the voices again.

"Yes, if no one claims him, he'll be very useful," he heard. "He's strong enough to pull the small cart, isn't he?"

Merrylegs started back, his hoofs going clickety-clack on the ground. Not be a

roundabout horse! Be made to pull a cart! He must get away—back to the farm. If he MUST pull a cart, he'd rather pull the farmer's than any other in the world! He pulled at the rope that fastened him to the wheel, he pulled again and again until a rough voice told him to keep still.

The little brown pony was afraid to move, and it was not long before he fell fast asleep. His eyes closed; his head dropped lower and lower; and he dreamt he was a roundabout horse.

His eyes flashed, and he was painted a beautiful scarlet. His front hoofs pawed the air, and his long mane and tail floated out behind him. How excited Merrylegs was when the loud music began, and crowds of children came running into the square. And now he was moving slowly round, with a little girl on his back.

Round and round he went, and faster and faster; and on and on went the music,

and soon Merrylegs began to feel a little queer. His head felt swimmy, and his tummy felt funny, and he began to wish he could stop. And stop he did, but only for a moment. Off he started again, with a little boy on his back. The music grew louder; it made his head ache. He felt very sick, and the little boy on his back thumped his head with his fist, and kicked him with his heels.

Was this how it felt to be a roundabout horse? How mistaken he had been . . . Oh, if only . . . and then he woke up.

It was quite light, and Merrylegs could hear a lark singing. Oh joy! He was himself, and not a roundabout horse after all. As he danced with pleasure, the man came out of the caravan and began to untie the rope fastened to the wheel.

"Now or never!" neighed Merrylegs, as he jerked the rope out of the man's hand, and galloped away down the road.

"Daisy and Squeaker were right after all," he thought as he went. "The farm is the best place . . . being a roundabout horse was horrid. I can't think how those red horses stand it. Why, I don't believe they are real horses after all. They are only made of wood. How silly I have been." And Merrylegs laughed at himself as he pushed his way through the gap in the hedge into his own field again.

Daisy heard him at once. She was very glad to see him back, and hurried off to tell Squeaker the good news. The farmer was very surprised next morning when he found his pony wearing a bridle.

Merrylegs was thankful to be at home again with his friends. He found that he quite enjoyed his work; in fact, he became so contented that after a time he even forgot all about his great-great-grandfather, the race horse.

Series 497